Femboy Evolution

- An LGBT, Femboy, First Time, Feminization, Short-Read Romance

by Barbara Deloto and Thomas Newgen

To purchase another copy of this book, or to see our other books go to
https://www.amazon.com/Barbara-Deloto/e/B00J21HWA4/

A few of our other books
Realizing Jessica - A Femboy Gets Fem and Discovers Inner Passions and Love
Desires- Fantasy Becomes Reality for an Occasional Crossdresser
Trannies - Two Guys Get Fem
Jessica's Turn: A Gender-Bending LGBT Romance
Frat House - A Gender-Bending LGBT Romance
Finishing School - A Boy Is Sent to a Girls' Finishing School - An LGBT Romance
All Dolled Up: A Student Gets Fem - An LGBT Romance
Sissy Boyfriend
Being Candy
Paying My Dues
Virtual Vacation
Filling in For Her
His New Dress
Her Gift to Him
Telling Her
Feminized to Win
Crossdreaming
Feminized by Her
Taking it for the Team
Feminized Men: A Guide for Increased Joy in Crossdressing
Feminized Vacation
The House of Enchanted Feminization
Heirs to Heiresses
Connected
Our Gift to Each Other
Girlfriend
Insatiable
A New Taste for Life
Spellbound
Femboy Guild

1

I cuddled next to Riley, whose hand slid gently on my thick, super soft, rainbow-striped, thigh-highs, squeezing my leg and making me feel cozy and sexy. "That feels so wonderful, Riley. Thank you."

"Come on, Avery, you know I'm just being selfish because I love doing it as much as you love feeling it."

"So true… mmm. Then as long as you're enjoying it, I guess I have to allow it. How could I ever deny you pleasure?" I gave a Riley a peck on the forehead. "So, buddy, what do we want to do on school break? I mean, what can we do to have some fun and make things more interesting? This is the last year we'll have so much time off before we go out into the crazy world of app development."

Riley slid off the couch and stretched. Painted nails went through fluffy, long, honey-colored hair and fluffed it more. "I say we go to the bar and see what the other femboys are up to. Maybe they have some ideas for break. I could wear my new girl jeans. You could wear those cute new boots you got. Why not wear your new skirt too?" Riley gave me an evil grin.

I laughed. "I wish. I wish we could do it all the way so I could present as a girl."

"Then do it, Avery."

"You should do it. You'd make a perfect girl. I love you when you're your most girly. But I'm concerned what the others would say. Aren't you?"

"C'mon, Avery. They're femboys. Do you think they'd care? They'd probably be jealous because you had the balls to be a girl. Just because we like to act somewhat androgynous, leaning toward the feminine, doesn't mean we can't act completely feminine."

I shrugged. "Hmm. Maybe. But my balls aren't that big tonight, or ever. You do it if you want. I'd love *you* to."

Riley's face flushed red, and he averted his eyes from mine. "Nah."

"Okay then. Let's just go and have a couple of drinks with them. I'm sure they're there by now." I stood and stretched then gave Riley a hug. I rubbed the front of his short shorts with one hand while I palmed his bottom and squeezed. "You're so sexy. You'd be the perfect girl. You have such a peachy butt."

Riley returned the caresses and breathed in my ear. "Oh yeah? See? You're acting like a girl—you're so hot for me and you're seducing me. Be my girlfriend tonight."

I sniffed Riley's sweet-smelling hair and wrapped my fingers in it, then mashed our glossed lips together and kissed him deeply. I whispered in his ear, "You'd make such a pretty girl, Riley. Why don't you wear a skirt tonight? Please? Maybe your sexy, strappy, stiletto bed-shoes too. Wear them out in public and scuff up the soles so you stop slipping on the carpet."

"Avery! You're making me crazy. I don't have the balls for it either, honey. Sorry. But you do. I know you do. They're right below that huge silky thing that always seems to be hard."

Riley slid his hand in my shorts and cupped my shaved globes, then dropped to his knees and looked up at me as he moved my short shorts to the side. "I need to take care of this obtrusive thing for you, Avery. Is that okay, sweetie?"

I nodded, looked down at his pretty eyes gazing up at me, and held his head gently.

2

Needless to say, as usual, I succumbed to Riley's ministrations. When I was almost at the end of my control, I tugged Riley to the floor with me and, as usual, we both utilized each other's pretty faces to deposit our overwhelming desires. It was, as usual, wonderful, but left us both feeling, as usual, somewhat disappointed for some reason.

Riley sprang up from the floor and licked his lips.

I tucked myself back into my shorts and then wiped a drip off my chin. "Thanks, Riley. I needed that to clear my head. Now we can go meet the other femboys without thinking about me presenting as a girl."

Riley shook his head. "You know that's why we both had to do that, right? It's because thinking of presenting as girls is exciting. We both wish the other was our girlfriend, and we both wish we were feminine and sexy and feeling pretty in girls' clothes, not boys' clothes. We want it—both for ourselves and for each other."

"Not me. Not now. I'm all better now that we got rid of those monkeys on our backs. I like being a femboy. It's perfect, and it fits who I am. I'm not a girl, and I can't think about presenting as one. It's not right."

"But it's okay to present as a feminine boy? That isn't exactly accepted in mainstream society either."

"Then you do it, Riley. Be the girl!" I shook my head and went into the bathroom to clean up, put on some mascara and eyeliner and a little bit of blusher and lip gloss.

I stared at myself in the mirror, fluffing my hair and putting some product in it. I looked into my eyes. My soul cried to me to do more makeup and turn myself into the girl of my dreams. I put it out of my mind and put on girls' jeans and my cute new girls' boots with the three-inch heels. They looked somewhat like a guys' boot but with a higher heel. The heels felt nice to walk in compared to sneakers or mocassins. I felt confident in them, and they looked and felt feminine and alluring.

When I came out, Riley was ready to go. His man-bag was slung on his shoulder as he loaded his things into it. His mascara and eyeliner were done, a nice, sweet cologne wafted around him, and his hair was in a ponytail. I kissed his cheek. "You smell delicious. Look great too."

"See? I make a handsome femboy. You, however, look really pretty." He slapped my bottom. "Girl!"

We both laughed. I slung my bag on my shoulder, grabbed his hand, and tugged him out of the house.

3

The bar on our street was great. It was a gay bar and felt warm and friendly. Nothing like those macho sports bars, where we'd have to masquerade as normal guys, trying to look tough in gross, disheveled clothes with no eyeliner or blush or lip gloss. I hated having to try to fit into those places. I always felt like an alien. Even at the regular bars at nice hotels, we'd have to dress in sport coats and ties, and we would both look like idiots trying to fit in. This bar was home for us.

"Riley! Avery! Come on over," Jamie called to us, waving a hand with painted nails from a table in the corner where he sat with another guy and a girl.

We went over and gave hugs and pecks on the cheek to them all. The girl was gorgeous in her V-neck minidress, stockings and heels, all made up with eyeshadow, eyeliner, and mascara. Her painted lips curved into a smile. She practically glowed, she was so pretty, and she seemed very familiar. I wanted to know what her perfume was so I could wear it at home. I wanted her outfit. I wanted her dangling earrings and long fake nails. I wanted her strappy stilettos. I wanted to be able to feel what she felt when she sat down and tucked the hem of her minidress under her. What she felt when her legs crossed each other in the sheer suntan pantyhose like they just had.

Riley tugged my arm and whispered in my ear. "Stop staring at her and sit down. You look like an idiot."

She gave me a flat-lipped, nervous smile, and I sat, still staring at her. She reached her hand out. "Hi Avery! I'm Alex." Her nervous smile turned to a nervous grin.

"Uh, Alex? I know an Alex. I..." I stared. She winked. "OMG! Alex! Wow! You're gorgeous, man... I mean... girl."

"Thanks. I had to do it. Glad you like it." She raised a limp wrist, fanning her long, painted nails. "I simply love it." She looked around then back at me and leaned toward me. Looking at me and smiling, she squeezed her breast. "Love these gel breasts and the great cleavage they give me, don't you?"

I nodded and stared at her cleavage.

She fluffed her hair. "Like this wig? I'm gonna grow my hair out and get a girl's cut and highlights from now on too. I'm done with just being a boring femboy. Do you think that's acceptable?"

Riley was nodding quickly as beers showed up for each of us and he put his hand out to Alex. "Let me shake your hand, man...uh, girl. We were just talking about doing what you did. Just for a night or over break maybe. You got balls, and you look great."

She shook his hand and laughed. "Yes, I do have a couple of those just like you two. Thanks for the compliments. You both have to do it! It's so darn liberating to be who you are inside. I feel like I died and went to heaven. To be out in public like this, and now, to have you guys and the rest of them here accepting and applauding me—I feel great." She looked around the table. "Thank you all for being so supportive."

I watched her cross and uncross her legs and bounce a foot in her heels. She caressed her sheer-stockinged leg and gave me doe eyes as she took my hand and rested it on her thigh. "You can't imagine how good this feels, Riley. You have to do it."

I slid my hand along her leg, imagining I was her, like I did with every pretty woman I saw. She was perfect. "Your voice matches so well."

"Just my regular voice. Well, maybe my polite voice. You know. Just a bit higher, like when you're being polite. Your voice and Avery's would be fine too. You two have got to do this, sweetie." She looked around the table. "We all should do this. Jamie, Ryan. Say you'll all do it. Let's all be the best girls we can over break. Why not? It'll be such fun. I know you all want to. Admit it." She sipped her martini, her gorgeous, made-up eyes looking across it at all four of us.

All of us looked away like nervous little kids trying to avoid their mother's stare after stealing her panties.

Alex laughed. "Look at you sissies. You look like I asked you all to strangle the cat." She laughed. "It's just clothes and makeup and it can all come off, but what it'll do for you is beyond superficial. I'm telling you it's femboy evolution, girls! You're all girls, and you know it. Stop masquerading and evolve into who you are. Trust me. You won't regret it." She finished her martini and raised her hand to order another.

We all looked at each other, gauging each other's reaction. Jamie crossed his legs, tented his painted nailed hands on the knee of his girl jeans, and bounced his foot in a girls' sneaker. He adjusted his bracelet and took a deep breath, his eyes flitting across all of us as he sipped his beer.

Alex took Jamie's hand in hers. "C'mon, princess. Be who you are. Join us." She squeezed his hand.

He squeezed back, then kissed her hand, murmuring "Mmm… Why not?" He nodded and raised his beer to us all. "To Alex freeing our minds. To us all becoming the girls we are." He let go of Alex's hand, which went right to his crotch and pressed between his legs. I could tell he was as excited by the thought as I was. I throbbed in my panties and saw Riley's face flush.

We all clinked glasses. Alex said, "To girls and liberty. Evolution of the femboys!"

We all drank. We ordered pizza and wings, and Riley and I ordered martinis. We all talked about what we could do over break as girls and what kind of excitement we could have. By the end of the night, we were all aroused, touchy-feely, and looking forward to our first outing together.

Riley and I left and walked arm in arm back to our place. When we were inside, we both put on the most feminine and sexiest things we owned. I wore my bed-shoes and Riley wore his, along with silky nighties and sheer, lace-top thigh-highs. We kissed and embraced and fell into each other in a mass of silkiness and perfume. We humped each other's legs, stroked each other's hardness slowly and sensually, talked about seducing men and controlling their passions, feeling their lust for us, driving them wild, and making them give us their passion.

We edged and played, sucked, stroked, and nibbled each other's shafts in sync, then lay together and gazed longingly into each other's eyes. Riley took both of our hardnesses into her soft little hand, and we both humped, rod to rod, as we kissed. We held off and kept changing our ministrations until we couldn't take it any longer, and then... looking into each other's eyes, we both slowly and torturously humped into the silky panties I wrapped around both of our shafts. Our breath was hot and choppy. Riley whispered, "Feel him in your hand, Avery. He wants to put it inside your pretty peach bottom and fill you with his release. Do you want him to?"

I nodded quickly. "God, yes."

"He will. You'll be his girl tonight. You'll be his depository."

"Do it for me, Riley. Take me like that, please?" I tried to maneuver to allow Riley access. He didn't let me.

"No. I have to be a girl too, remember? Just imagine it. Imagine a hunk with you as his girl for the night."

I slid the panties against us both, feeling Riley's hard shaft rubbing mine as he humped slowly against my shaft and into my pantie-covered hand.

Riley narrated again, "He'll be thrusting it into you, Avery. He'll be fervent like an animal because you excite him so much... like this." He held my hand tight and thrusted fast and hard, rubbing against my shaft and slipping the panties against us in my now crushing grip as he made deep-throated, bestial grunts.

Riley's voice went high, and he mewled. I let out a whimper like a little girl as I felt his shaft swell and shrink and flood us both with his release. My body clenched, and I shot—knees twitching, high heels kicking, breathless squeals and gushes in time with his. When we stopped shaking, we fell apart, our wet shafts resting and moving slowly against each other's silky sheer-stockinged legs.

Riley kissed my forehead. "You're a beautiful girl, Avery."

"You are too, princess. I know you were just playing the role of the man for us... for the story. I can tell the story was for you as much as for me. It's what you want too, isn't it?"

"Maybe. It's exciting as hell to think of. I love how you react to it. How excited it gets you and how good it makes you feel, Avery. I love you so much. Be my girlfriend. Please?"

I nodded and started to tear up. "I love you too, Riley. I'll be your girlfriend if you'll be mine." I hugged her tight to me. She was my girl now, and I was hers. I felt liberated, evolved.

4

In the morning, we woke with Riley spooning me. I pressed my pantie-clad bottom back against his hardness. His hot breath fell on my neck as he let out a little, girly moan. I rolled over and slid my leg between his, our stockings gliding against one another, our shoes slipping their long sharp heels across our legs. I humped against his silk-bound shaft with mine. I looked into his eyes. "I want to get gel breast forms. I want cleavage like Alex's."

That comment sped up Riley's humping, and he ran his hand over my hair as he gazed at me. "That sounds delicious to me too. I want to get my hair done properly. I want highlights and layers and sexiness. I want long fake nails and a gel pedicure. I want extra sheer stockings and pantyhose and sexy minidresses and skirts and cleavage-revealing tops."

I humped faster thinking about both of us like that. "Oh god, yes, Riley. We'll be two hot, sensual women." I came profusely on us both, and Riley let out a whimper as he lost control as well. We crushed each other while we shook and shuddered until it stopped. We fell onto our backs, and Riley took my hand as we caught our breaths.

He said in her polite voice, "Wow, girl. It's better already just thinking about being girls. Last night and this morning were the best sex I ever had. I can't wait to finally be the sensual, feminine, lovely creature I always wanted to be. I hope I'm not a disappointment to myself."

I rolled over and rested on my elbow. I ran my fingers through her hair and kissed her cheek. "Oh, girl, you won't be a disappointment. I know. Let's take a shower together, then help each other with our makeup. We need to go to breakfast and go shopping for clothes and things and get our hair and nails done. We have a very busy day... girl."

5

"You look great, Avery," Riley said as we both checked ourselves out in the full-length mirror—our makeup done, perfumed, hair styled, earrings dangling. We wore bras and panties under our girl jeans and tank tops with open blouses.

I nodded. "I guess this is as good as we can do for now, girl. Thanks for helping with the makeup. I never really used eyeshadow or blusher much. You did a great job contouring my face, and the eyeshadow changes everything. I love it. Thank you." So as not to mess up my lips gloss, I kissed my finger and placed it on her forehead.

"Quite welcome." Riley fussed with her high ponytail, trying to fluff it out behind her. "I have to get this hair done." She turned to me and checked me up and down. "No one will ever know. We're perfect. Let's go complete our evolution." She slung her purse on her shoulder, as did I. She took my hand and we left.

Our first stop was of course the salon—new hair do's, highlighting, layering. Riley left hers down to her shoulder with added curls and highlights, and I had mine cut to just over my collar in a wild, shaggy style, with blonde-to-reddish-brown highlights.

We had our pedicures done with light pink nail gel and matched them with extra-long, curved, French-cut acrylic nails. It was interesting trying to get our credit cards out of our wallets with our new nails. They made me feel so feminine, but we had to learn how to deal with them. It was a challenge we were both enjoying.

Next stop, we both bought gel breast forms that fit our torsos without being excessive but that allowed for maximum cleavage and substantial weight. We wore them out of the store with the new bras we bought, along with other bras, panties, garter belts, thigh-high stockings, pantyhose, and nightwear.

The breasts tugged and pulled with each step, giving me the illusion that they were real. I throbbed in my panties from the sensuality of it all. I felt I was a real girl at that point.

Our next stop was for shoes. We both went for the highest heels we could find in strappy styles. Stilettos, wedge heels, boots, and mules. We had to haul all our purchases back to the car before we could continue, and we both wore new high-heel boots with our skinny jeans tucked in as we continued our shopping.

Costume jewelry, minidresses, miniskirts, and halter and V-neck tops and sweaters. Crop-tops, scarves, coats, fingerless gloves... There was nothing feminine we didn't buy. We were beside ourselves with excitement. My heart raced all day as we tried on different clothes. I couldn't wait to go out in public in all our new and wondrous finds. It was so much better than the clothing restrictions imposed on males. Liberating was an understatement!

When we had exhausted our shopping options, we dragged the last of our purchases to the car and loaded them in the only available space, in the back seat. I flopped into the passenger seat and slugged from my water bottle. Riley got in her side and flopped her head back against the head rest. "God! That was good. I finally know why women shop till they drop. It was fantastic." She clasped my hand with hers and smiled at me, her new hair looking fabulous.

I leaned over and kissed her lightly on the lips. "Yes, thank you for doing this with me. I'm so glad we took this step."

"Me too."

"Let's go home and put our things away, wash a few of them, then get dressed and go out for a fancy dinner."

"What about the other girls? Shouldn't we check on Jamie, Ryan, and Alex? I'd love to see how Jamie and Ryan turned out. I'm sure Alex helped them too."

Riley shrugged. "I guess. I just want to get dressed the way I always dreamed of and be with you to enjoy a nice evening together. It's been a hell of a day already. Do we really want to be social?"

"True. But don't we want to find some real men to fulfill our fantasies?" I reached over and rubbed Riley's hardness in her jeans. "I mean, maybe we could go and find some straight guys."

She removed my hand from her pants and squeezed it. "Uh, straight guys wouldn't be wanting to do us, honey. They might beat us up."

"Hmm, maybe. Maybe not, though. Well, how about the gay bar? There are some really handsome guys there who look straight."

"They might go for us, but those guys usually like guys, not girls. I mean we could try it, but I'm really not in the mood for anyone but you right now. I want to relax and enjoy my girlfriend, Avery... okay?"

"Okay. I'll make a reservation somewhere while you drive. Something quiet and romantic?"

"Sounds great."

I found a place and made the reservation. I looked out the window while Riley drove, and I throbbed in my jeans. I ran my long nails up and down my crossed leg, thinking about some of the guys we could have. I closed my eyes and remembered the narration Riley did for us the night before. I had to stop bouncing my leg or I'd wet my jeans.

"You okay, Avery? What are you thinking of?"

"Oh nothing. Just relishing being a girl, that's all."

6

We completed our tasks, washing and drying some of our new things and putting away our purchases, and then we chose and laid out our clothes and accessories for dinner. We had an hour and a half left before our reservation. I wrapped my arms around Riley from behind and kissed her neck. "Want some iced tea and an emergency smoke before we get ready?"

"Sure." She turned around and gave me a big hug and kiss on my lips. She leaned back and looked at me. "I'm bushed. If I weren't so excited to have a romantic evening out as a girl with my new girlfriend, I'd just flop on the couch in some cozy thigh-highs and short shorts and eat pizza and fall asleep on a chick flick."

I laughed. "Yeah, our normal chilling-out standard. I'm sure we'll get there again sometime. We might be dressed better than that, though. Those clothes sound so boring now."

"True. Let's go take that break and get ready."

After our little break, we each showered and shaved our bodies smooth and silky. We redid our makeup for a more dramatic evening look and got dressed. I was in heaven as I wrapped the garter belt around my waist, slid the gossamer-thin, silky black stockings up my smooth and sensitive legs, and attached the garters. I then slid up the stretchy satin and black lace panties and tucked my rigid shaft into them. I slid black ruffled garters with pearls on them above the stockings.

I put on a matching bra, filled it with the forms, and adjusted my cleavage in it. I slid up the black chiffon V-neck minidress and zipped the back and adjusted my cleavage again. Next, I fastened five-inch black patent leather strappy stilettos securely around my ankles. Matching gold and silver ankle bracelets brought the eye to the curve of my ankle.

I loaded on bracelets, a necklace, and new dangling earrings in both holes in each ear. I and sprayed myself with perfume, which I put in my purse along with my lipstick, blush, eyeliner, and mascara just in case. I slipped a handful of lubricated condoms in the side pocket and put my license and credit cards in the new wallet and into the purse. I wrapped a sheer shawl over my bare shoulders and put the ends though a silver ring just below my breasts and tied it off. I checked myself in the mirror.

"Stunning, dear. Absolutely stunning. Total eye candy." Riley leaned down and kissed my cheek lightly. "I'd be so proud as a man to have you on my arm." She stood alongside me, holding my hand as we both smiled into the full-length mirror. She was a few inches taller than me and looked regal and graceful in her black velvet minidress, her cleavage emphasized by the silver heart pendant resting between her breasts.

"You look fabulous, Riley. So regal and graceful."

"Thanks. You don't think I'm too tall in these heels? Your five-four height can handle the stilettos. I'm not sure my five-six height works. I might get clocked."

"Nonsense! You're just a statuesque girl. Look at yourself in the mirror and tell me you don't look one hundred percent female. You just need a nice tall man by your side to balance your height, that's all. And you know what else nice tall men have, honey. Nice big... mmm. Yes. Nice big, long, hard impalers to fill your peachy bottom to your throat. Just imagine being his girl."

Riley stared at herself in the mirror like she saw a ghost.

I took her arm in mine. "C'mon, honey. Relax. Let's go have a nice romantic dinner."

7

On the ride to the restaurant, I managed to calm Riley down a little by giving her some attention under her dress with my mouth while she drove. I didn't allow it to get out of hand, though, so she could feel the sensuality of her new self throughout the night. Doing so sure did make me feel sensual and sexy as well, and I wondered if I did it as much for myself as I did for her. We were tucked away again and fully presentable when the valet opened our doors and took the car away.

The restaurant was lovely with thick, quiet carpets, soft classical music, and a fireplace by our table. The place smelled heavenly, with wonderful aromas emanating from the kitchen. The maître d' seated us at adjacent corners of the table facing the fireplace. There were only a few other couples at the spread-out tables and a waiter by the far wall with a white towel over one arm of his tux, waiting to serve. He made his way to us with a tray and water glasses.

"Welcome, ladies. My name's Pierce, and I'll be taking care of you this evening." He opened drink menus and put them before us. "May I bring you a drink before dinner? If you haven't tried the cherry martini, I highly recommend it. It's called a lady's passion. It isn't exceptionally sweet. Just enough cherry juice for the color. It's served with an edible flower float that is quite pretty and tasty." He stood with his hands clasped behind his back, smiling at us.

Riley was reading the menu. I looked up at the tall handsome Pierce and couldn't help glancing at the long straight ripple by the crotch of his pants from his obvious endowment. It was flaccid, and it was that big! He caught me looking, and when I looked up at him, he grinned. "Miss? See something you like?"

My face flushed. I looked at the menu. "Uh, yes I did. Very nice as a matter of fact. Really, really nice." I laughed a little and felt myself blush. "I think I'd like to have the passionate release. I mean..." I looked back at the menu. "I mean... I'd like a lady's passion. The martini that is." My face had to have been beet red.

"Of course, miss. Good choice. All ladies must satisfy their passion." He turned to Riley. "And you, miss? Have you decided, or would you like more time?"

Riley looked up from the menu. "That sounds pleasant. I'll have one too, please." She put the menu down.

"Very good choice, ladies. You won't be disappointed." He picked the menus up and left.

I placed my hand on Riley's sheer-stockinged leg and caressed her thigh as I leaned into her and whispered, "Did you see the outline of Pierce's meat? It would be one hell of a piercing for sure. I couldn't imagine having that thing inside me. It would be heaven."

Riley crossed her legs, slid my hand off her leg and held it. "Go for it, dear. I caught you looking at it. It's ginormous, and it isn't even grown."

"You should go for it, Riley. A guy the size of Pierce is exactly what a girl your size needs. You'd be a perfect match."

She rolled her eyes. "Oh Avery, stop. Please. I just want to be with you and enjoy our new presentation. Can you just stop for a minute and enjoy us?" She slid her long-nailed hand on my stockinged thigh. "Please?"

"I'm sorry. I didn't mean to upset you. Of course. It's just us now. I'll stop."

"Thank you."

Pierce came back with the drinks. This time he was partially hard under his pants. It was fabulous. He winked at me as he left my cocktail. A smile covered my face ear to ear. "Thank you for that presentation, Pierce. It's so... impressive!" I picked up the martini by the stem and held it to admire it. "It's edible too?"

"Yes, miss. You're welcome to take it into your lovely mouth and crush it between your tongue and the roof, where it will gush its juices and please your palate with a reward of a luscious release. Please indulge as you wish."

He turned to Riley, who was looking down at the drink. "Everything okay, miss?"

She looked up, her face red. "Uh, yes. Thank you for that vivid description." She uncrossed and recrossed her legs, pressing down between them momentarily as she adjusted the hem with the other hand and wriggled in her seat. He smiled at her and left.

Riley took the flower from the drink and placed it in her mouth, as did I. We looked at each other as we crushed it and tasted it. Something creamy and flavorful burst like a capsule in the flower and flooded over our tongues. Riley's eyes went wide.

I nodded. "Wow! There was a flavor capsule in there. That was fantastic. Just like he said."

"It was. That was fun. I wasn't expecting that. Must be some new drink trick." She held her martini out, clasping it in her long-nailed fingers, her pink nails glinting in the light. "To my forever girlfriend."

"And mine." We both sipped down a good amount and placed the glasses on the table. "Nice. Love the light cherry flavor. Not too sweet either."

"Agreed. So, Avery. My love. Are you going to suck off Pierce before the night's over, or are you going to trick him into thinking you're a real girl who has her period and have him screw your butt in the ladies' room?"

I looked around then glared at her. "Riley!"

"I know you want it." She sipped her drink, bouncing a leg over the other. "Go for it, Avery."

"I, uh. I... no."

"No? It's your fantasy, Avery."

"You *narrate* it, Riley. It's *your* fantasy. *You* do Pierce. I'll watch."

"I don't want a man as much as you do. Go for it. I just want you... my girlfriend."

"Let's not talk about this. We're supposed to be enjoying each other, and you're making things all tense, and I'm losing my libido. I'm starting to feel less sensual and pretty. I'm sure you're not feeling very good right now either. I think you're jealous."

"I'm not. I want what you want. I mean... for you, that is. I want you to have your dream come true." She stared blankly at me. I could tell she was upset. She wasn't happy at all.

I took her hand in mine on the table and leaned into her. I looked into her made-up eyes. "I love you. That's all that matters. Let's enjoy ourselves like we wanted to. God knows this dinner is going to cost a pretty penny. We could have bought more clothes and shoes with all the money this will cost, so let's not waste it being upset. I promise not to dwell on Pierce if you don't keep prodding me to go for him."

"Prodding?" She rolled her eyes.

"Riley. Please?" I squeezed her hand and caressed her thigh. "Please? I just want to enjoy us." I slid my hand on her leg and gazed into her eyes.

"Okay. I'll stop. It's my fault, too, for getting jealous and catty." She took a deep breath and gazed lovingly at me. "Okay. I'm done."

"Me too." I leaned in and gave her a peck on her lips, then slid the hem of my dress under me again and crossed my legs so one slid against hers. "I love you."

"Me too." She pecked my lips and squeezed my hand. She lifted her drink. "Let's finish these so we can get another creamy gush of flavor. To passionate releases for both of us."

"Oh my god, yes, girl!" I clinked and we drank them down. Pierce was by the table in a moment, his crisp, white towel over his arm and covering the crotch of his pants. He placed a menu before Riley, and she held it out before her.

Pierce moved his toweled arm aside as he took the drinks from the table. It was harder and longer beneath his pants. I couldn't stop looking at it; it actually throbbed while Riley stared at the menu, and I ordered two more drinks. Pierce winked and covered his display with his towel as he turned and left, no one else the wiser to his arousal.

I throbbed uncontrollably in my panties, and Riley caressed my thigh sensually while she looked over the food menu he had brought. I pressed my hard shaft and trapped it between my crossed legs. Riley kept caressing me as she perused the menu. She squeezed my leg. "This is nice now, isn't it, honey? Just you and me immersed in our wonderful femininity, sensuality, and fine drinks and food. No distractions. This menu is incredible, isn't it? I want it all."

I nodded and caressed her leg while she caressed mine. "Yes, honey. I want it all too."

I looked across the room. Pierce smiled from the far wall and nodded.

8

We ate like we'd never eaten before. Each course was a culinary delight. Maybe it was because we were both dressed so femininely and sensually, and our senses were ablaze with it all. Maybe it was just a great restaurant, but we'd had similar meals there before and never enjoyed them so much—the aromas, the tastes, the textures on the tongue, the vibrance of every nuance.

In between courses, we'd touch and caress each other discreetly. Riley talked about what a lovely girlfriend I was and how much she loved me. It was so romantic, and I felt loved and alive.

The only thing that distracted me a bit was when Pierce cleared or brought courses. He was adept at making sure I could see things and Riley couldn't. He knew how interested I was in him, and he took advantage of that.

He stood while Riley perused the dessert menu, and he managed to flash from under his towel, and this time, smoothly shaven, terribly intimidating in size, it was standing proudly up to his waist, topped with a big purplish head. He winked and grasped it with his big hand and waved it like a sword, then put it away before Riley was any the wiser.

I covered my mouth with my hand and almost gave out a squeal. I checked, and Riley was engrossed in the menu. She hadn't seen. My heart raced and my face flushed. I tried to stop my approving grin with no luck. Pierce winked and nodded.

Riley looked up from the menu at me. "I can't decide, Avery. You pick and we can share, okay?"

"Sure honey. Pierce, what would you recommend?"

"The bananas foster is wonderful. We have fantastic bananas here. Plenty of long, thick, sweet, and firm banana meat to share, generously oozing with luscious cream, caramel, and ice cream. It represents the fine payoff after the evening's alluring and tantalizing sensory buildup." He gave us a crooked grin.

I throbbed and a shiver ran through me. I recrossed my legs and tucked it between my thighs, licked my lips, and said, "Sounds... uh... very inviting. I can't wait for the payoff." I handed him our menus and he left. I wiped sweat from my brow with my napkin and recrossed my legs, trapping it again, and bounced a foot, squeezing it with each bounce.

Riley took my hand in hers. "You're sweating, sweetie. Are you hot?"

"Just a little. All the food, I guess."

"Right. There was a lot of food. Sounds like quite an interesting dessert. Sounds as good as sex."

I gave Riley a flat-lipped smile, then looked around. Pierce was evidently in the kitchen.

Riley slid her hand between my legs, and her finger found the tip of my hardness, revealing my mental state. She smiled. "Mmm, nice."

"Yes. How about you?"

"Just a bit. Not really rigid, though. Just comfy and nice." She ran her hands on her thighs and took a deep breath, then sighed. "You know, I really think you should take advantage of Pierce. I mean, he hadn't been making the remarks and stuff until that dessert description, and he's been hiding his scenic view with his towel, but from the way he's been acting, I'll bet he'd jump at the chance to have you. I think he wants you."

"Riley!" I throbbed in my panties uncontrollably again, imagining Pierce in me. My foot bounced. My hands caressed my silky stockinged thighs unconsciously. My body tingled. "No. I don't want to."

"Don't lie, girl. I see it in your body language. Your face is glowing like a bride on her honeymoon. Do it. Do it or I'll get angry and won't play with you for a week."

"What? How could you?"

"Avery. Just do it. Step up to your desires. Be honest with yourself."

"He might beat me up or something if he finds out I'm not real."

"I can take care of that so it's safe."

"How? You have a gun?"

"No, silly. I'll take care of it, though. Just tell me you'll do Pierce. I want it for you. Please?"

I took a deep breath and looked for any signs of hesitation, jealousy, or manipulation from her. She was sincere. She did want it for me. That didn't mean it wouldn't cause problems later, but right now she wanted it. I wanted it even more. Still, I shook my head.

She whined, "Please? Please let me give you this gift. I know it's your fantasy."

"What will you do?"

"I can be there if you want, and I'll watch, or you can be alone with him."

"Watch? You should be getting some of it too."

"I don't want it like you do, but I do want to make you happy and give you this."

"How can you?"

Our bananas foster arrived. I covered my mouth with my hand and gasped. It was a huge banana cut in half with the two ends made to stand erect with caramel and cream dripping from the tips, which were carved with holes in each and a head like a penis. Small scoops of ice cream took the place of the balls on each. Pierce placed it between us. "Voila! Our chef is an artist, isn't he? If it offends you, you can just knock it down to eat it."

I looked up at Pierce, his gleaming dark, smiling eyes, his smoothly shaved face, his perfectly combed hair. A whiff of fresh cologne came off him. "Yes, lovely, Pierce. Thank you."

He smiled and left. We dug in, laughing as we did. When we had finished and were sipping our espressos, Riley abruptly took her purse and went over to Pierce. I watched as she talked to him. Pierce's eyes went wide; he looked Riley up and down. He kissed his fingertips as if saying that was wonderful, then he looked over at me. He nodded quickly to Riley and looked at his watch and then whispered in her ear. She took a credit card out of her purse and gave it to him. She walked back, her hips swaying, her breasts jiggling, a smile ear to ear.

She daintily slid her dress under her and sat, crossed her legs, and bounced a foot. "Done. Told him what we were. He loves it and wants to take care of you." She took my hand. "I'm so excited for you, sweetie."

"Really? No way."

"Way. He's going to get the check. I'll pay for it. He said not to leave a tip because you would be tip enough."

"I'm beside myself. Wow." My heart was pounding in my chest. "Oh, Riley. I'm so scared now. I never thought all our fantasizing would become real."

"Don't be scared, girlfriend." She ran her hand on my thighs. "Relax."

I whispered in a whiny, choked-up voice, "He's soo big!"

"I know—isn't it great?"

"No. It might not fit. It might hurt me."

"No way. Remember some of the things we've had in you? I think we have a strap-on bigger than him that you had me wear."

"True. I do love when you wear it too." I remembered how much. I rolled my eyes. "And you're okay with this?"

"I set it up for you, girl."

The check came. Pierce smiled and winked at me. "See you ladies soon... I hope."

Riley watched me. I looked at her, then at Pierce, and he left. My face flushed. I checked my purse for the condoms. I grasped Riley's hand and gazed into her eyes. "You sure, honey? You sure you won't get jealous or angry or feel bad about something or other after?"

Riley gazed lovingly at me and swallowed hard. She struggled a bit then said, "No. We have to do this. You need to do this. So, alone with Pierce or with me there?"

"Oh god. With you. Please."

Riley signed the check and closed the booklet. "Then are you ready, young lady?"

I nodded and gauged her expression. I throbbed in my panties, and my body began to tingle all over as Riley gently rubbed the back of my hand with her long-nailed thumb. I wanted it so badly. Pierce was the man in my fantasies. I watched Riley carefully. Her eyes gazed lovingly at me with anticipation. Right now, she was truly excited for me to have this.

"Avery?"

"Yes. Uh..." I looked around.

9

Our visit to the ladies' room, taking care of business and touching up our makeup and hair and freshening our perfume, was complete.

I slung my hand on my purse and stood before Riley. It took everything in me to say it, but I did. I had to give Riley an out if she wanted it. I didn't want to hurt her. "Okay. Let's go home, honey."

Riley held me by the shoulders and looked into my eyes. "I won't let you not do this. You're ready. You want it very badly, I can tell. Don't lie to me. Tell me what you want, Avery. Tell me the truth."

I rolled my eyes and looked up at the ceiling. I whispered. "I want it."

"Want what?"

"I want... Pierce."

"To do what with?"

"Oh god, Riley. Don't make me say it."

"You have to say it. You have to be honest, or it will be all wrong."

"I rolled my eyes. "Okay. I admit it. I want Pierce to fill me up from my bottom to my throat and release all of his passion into me."

"Good girl. Let's go now." She dragged me by the arm out of the ladies' room.

I knelt on the pillow in the storage room and forced Riley to the floor beside me. I held the base of Pierce's huge man meat in one hand and moved Riley's head to place it against her lips. She closed her eyes and immediately became fervent in her pursuit of indulging in Pierce. "Good girl, Riley. Isn't it fabulous?" I looked up as Pierce rested a big hand on Riley's head and smiled down at us. I tugged on his shaved globes and rolled them in my palm while Riley indulged.

Pierce grasped her head with both hands and forcibly removed her from his shaft, then grabbed my chin and placed the thick head against my lips, which opened instinctively to greedily receive it as far into my wide-open mouth as I could.

My jaw was so far open I thought it might get stuck that way, but I ardently worked my tongue around his shaft and tip while bobbing my head on it. I stroked the lower section with both hands and watched the expression on his face—those dark eyes gazing fondly at me. It was so thick, firm, silky, and filling.

I loved the richness of it against my tongue and lips, the power within it that I knew I had created. I tasted the oozing cream and realized if I wasn't careful, I'd never get what I really wanted from this horse-sized impaler.

As much as I didn't want to remove it from my mouth, I wanted it more elsewhere. I wanted it in a place where I could fully receive its energy and be intimately connected to it.

I slid one hand into a small back pocket of my purse and felt for the extra-large condom package I'd never had the opportunity to use. I removed my other hand while Pierce held my head firmly and thrusted into my face. I tore open the package and looked up at him, showing him the open condom.

Holding my head tighter, he continued to thrust into my face up to the lipstick mark I'd left on his shaft. I tried to shake my head, my jaw wide open, my eyes wide open in fear he would finish and leave me empty down there, but he held my head firm in his grip, his eyes intent on mine. He shook his head, telling me no. He was careful that his rapid thrusts went only as far as the lipstick ring. I was lost in bliss at it all, but I didn't want to lose my more desired goal.

My hands were behind my back, as I tried not to offer any other stimulation, but my tongue couldn't resist circling it over and over. How could I ever stop him from shortchanging me of what I really wanted? I looked into his eyes and whimpered around his luxurious thunderbolt of energy.

His hands nearly crushed my skull, and then his provocation swelled and shrank in my hungry mouth as a gush went through it. I struggled to swallow it all, and he pulled back enough so I could. Then he shot load after load into my face as I looked into his dark eyes, his fingers wrapped tight in my hair. My body tingled all over, and I throbbed uncontrollably in my panties.

When he was done flooding my face, he pulled it out, and a last rope flung into my hair. He lifted me up, smiling at me. "Don't worry, my lady. You can have your cake and eat it too. I'm ready for dessert. Are you ready, sweet girl?" I nodded feverishly. He took the condom from my hand and sheathed his torpedo in it.

Pierce lifted me up onto the table in the storage room, my arms wrapped around his neck. I peeked over his shoulder at Riley as she stood with our purses on her shoulder and nodded her approval. Pierce called to her. "Miss, can you help get us started?" He lifted the hem of my minidress. I felt his rigid member pressing against my leg. He pulled my panties off and dropped them on the floor. My shaved little sailor sprang up and bobbed. "So cute and girlish," Pierce said as he pushed my legs back and pressed forward. He turned to Riley. "Miss? Can you guide me into her?"

Riley reached between us and grasped Pierce's shaft in her fist, guiding it and rubbing it against me, spreading the lube on the condom onto the target. I tried to wriggle onto it while Riley held it firmly, and Pierce's and my eyes locked as he pushed and stretched me open. The thick head stretched me. I gasped and whimpered, and he stopped. "No, no! Please, Pierce. Push."

He watched my expression, and I took a deep breath as it spread me and spread me until I thought I would rip open, then it made it past the gate and entered me. I gasped and held fast to Pierce's neck, peeking past him at Riley who was watching intently. What was the expression on her face? A look of awe? Fear? Her eyes were wide, locked on Pierce's shaft as it made its way inch by inch, deeper and deeper into me.

My heart pounded in my ears. When he was all the way in, he kissed my neck and breathed in my perfume. "So sweet! Such a sweet young lady you are." I could smell his cologne. He held my hips and slowly began thrusting almost all the way out and then back in. He sped up until he achieved a rhythmic, body-shaking pace.

I oozed from my bobbing shaft continually, and it felt as if it were one continuous finish, my skin tingling, my legs spasming, my high heels flailing, my body electric. Rather than a few gushes and done, it was a continual ride at the peak sensation as if the normal resulting gush of release had turned into a faucet.

I glanced at Riley as she leaned back against a table, watching Pierce thrusting into me over and over, faster and faster. Her hand with its long, painted nails covered her mouth, her eyes wide.

I turned my attention back to Pierce. He held me like a blow-up doll, my weight insignificant to him as he pummeled me. I gasped and whimpered, my body electrified by an enduring crescendo. I stroked his black hair and hung onto his neck with both hands. "Pierce, finish in me, you beautiful beast. I can't take much more. It feels too good and I might die."

He grasped me tight and rammed me over and over, his eyes wide; quiet, breathy grunts came from him as he looked into my eyes. All of a sudden, he shoved hard and held it there. I felt it swell inside me and flood into me. He pulled it back and shoved hard again while I uncontrollably released all the remaining pent-up passion from my little flailing and jerking sailor onto my belly.

He grunted and shoved over and over until he nearly dropped me. Then, while my sailor was still flailing and shooting blanks, my legs spasming like my little rod, he slid it out and gently lowered me to the table. He placed a kiss on my forehead, then began trying to tuck himself away, the condom filled and dangling a large white pouch at the end.

Riley handed me my panties, which she had picked up and kept in her purse. I slid them on while she wiped Pierce's first string of pearls from my hair with a tissue. Pierce held the door for us. "It's been a pleasure to serve you ladies this evening. Please. Come back. I'll take good care of you both if you like. Ask for me."

Red-faced and somewhat embarrassed, we left and went to the ladies' room to check ourselves hurriedly before we saw the valet. I slid into the car, and he closed the door behind me. Riley slipped him a tip and got in. We drove off.

I reclined the back of my seat, my legs spread unfemininely before me, my hands resting on my crotch.

"You okay, Avery?" She reached over and squeezed my hand.

"Oh god, yes." I looked at the ceiling of the car, the shadows moving as we passed streetlights. "That felt so heavenly. Nothing I ever did ever felt so divine. It was as if I were beside myself, and my body was entirely his huge masterpiece. It was as if I was his luscious extremity. My whole body felt like it. I was so connected to him, I could have been him, or just his shaft, but I wasn't. I was a woman pleasing her man. My pleasure came from him and was his." I caressed myself and took my hardening shaft out of my panties and began stroking it with the fabric of my dress. I closed my eyes and leaned my head back.

"I was just his passion, his sensation, his bestial release into me. Feeling him release in me, the way he swelled and pulsed deep inside me, was like receiving a gift from an animal god. I was a woman. A bride injected and embraced, enveloped with a real male's power and animal lust. I became his sensations consummately. I wonder if genetic women ever get to feel that. You have to do it, Riley. You have to."

I couldn't help stroking myself with the silky fabric of my dress. I closed my eyes and remembered it all.

"Wow. That good, huh, Avery?" Her voice was choppy.

"Yes. Incredible. You have to experience it." I continued stroking myself, remembering each moment, each thrust, the sensations throughout my body, my breaths getting deeper.

"Good. I'm very... uh, happy... you were able to experience that. Experience having a real man who could satisfy your deep feminine needs."

"Mmm... huh, uh, oh god, yes..." I furiously jerked myself, reliving it. "Oh Pierce, honey. Yes, that's it, baby, use me to fulfill your passion. Breed me. Use me for your pleasure so I can feel it too."

Riley squeezed my hand tight, then lifted it and dropped it. Her voice choppy, she said, "I love you, Avery."

"Uh, huh... huh! Ungh!... Huh... uh...." I stretched my legs out and crossed them as I yanked myself with thumb and forefinger, my pinky held out daintily, poking into the silky, slippery fabric of my dress. "Uh, huh, oh god, Pierce! Pierce, give me your love! Fill me. Huh, huh, uh." I shot a short squirt, and the other eight spasms shot nothing but shook my legs. I took a deep breath, my hand resting around my dress-wrapped, tired, and spent little friend. I fell fast asleep.

10

"Pierce, yes, honey!" I whispered against my sheets in my half-dazed, morning-wood, unconscious fervor. My pillow had gotten between my legs. I slipped and slid my high heels and stockings against the satin sheets, all my clothes still on from the night before. I rubbed against the pillow through my silky panties and sped up as I remembered the night before in the morning fog of my dreams. I heard myself call to him. "Huh, uh, oh god, Pierce."

I pressed the pillow together tightly around my twinky and humped into it like an adolescent. In seconds, I released into the satin panties and pillow. "Oh god yes, Pierce," I whispered as I shuddered.

It wasn't anywhere near as good as the actual thing, but it was sufficient for me to satisfy my longing momentarily. I rolled onto my back and saw Riley as her form sped from the room like a thief. I caught my breath, stripped my clothes off and went into the bathroom for my morning duty. The soreness I felt as I completed my duty reminded me again that I'd had a beast in that part of me last night.

I moved Riley's towel from the shower to the rack and placed mine on the shower. I cleaned out my bottom carefully and gently, washed and shaved my body, and shampooed and conditioned my hair. I dried and styled my lovely new hair and did my makeup. I loved seeing the girl looking back at me instead of the boring old me. I knew I was a girl entirely.

I moisturized my body and then got dressed in sheer suntan pantyhose, pink lace bra and panties, denim miniskirt with a pink V-neck sweater and high-wedge, beige-twine heels. I chose earrings and jewelry, sprayed perfume all over, and went into the kitchen. I walked up behind Riley, who was cooking bacon, and wrapped my arms around her from behind and hugged her, kissing her neck beneath her tight bun of hair. "Morning, my love. Thank you for last night. It was wonderful."

She turned around to face me. "Glad you enjoyed it." She turned back to the bacon.

I looked closer at her. "Riley, you're wearing your old boy jeans and boots and a lumberjack's plaid shirt, and your hair is in a man-bun in back. You can't even tell you had it wave permed and styled. Why are you wearing stud earrings when we bought so many pretty dangling ones?"

She lifted the bacon from the pan onto paper towels. "It's what I wanted today."

"Why?"

She took French toast out of the oven and put it on our plates, added the bacon, and delivered it all to the table. "Sit and eat, Avery. You must be famished from all your sex with Pierce last night, and with Pierce in the car, and with Pierce this morning."

She sat, as did I. I sipped the juice, then the coffee, and I poured maple syrup on the French toast. I watched as Riley prepared her food. No eyeliner, no mascara, bare lips, no makeup. She looked like a guy. Not even a femboy.

"Riley, you look like a guy. What's up? Why aren't you a girl today? What's wrong?"

"You're a girl today, Avery. You do look wonderful, by the way." She gave me a flat-lipped smile. "Very pretty."

"Thank you." I ate my toast, watching him. "So, why are you masquerading as a guy?"

"Well, you like being a girl, right?"

"Of course. I'm never going back to being a femboy. I've evolved."

"Yes. You've become a wonderful girl. A natural. Exactly as it should be. As you should be."

"Yes. So why aren't you? You're a perfect girl too."

Riley nodded. "I know. But now I realize that won't work."

"Why?"

"Because you need a real man in your life. I want to be that for you."

"Oh, Riley. Don't be silly. You could never be a real man. You never were, for gosh sakes." I laughed. "A femboy being a real man? Don't be ridiculous. Now after we eat, I want you to go dress like the girl you are. Fix that hair and do your makeup like a good girl."

"No. I'm going to be your boyfriend so I can fill your feminine needs. I can do it. You'll see."

It hit me. How could I miss it? My voice shook. "Pierce did this to you. I knew I shouldn't have done it. I mean I tried to stop it, but you insisted, and then you even helped stick him in me, and you loved watching me when he came in me. You covered your mouth seeing how glorious it was. I did it because that was what you wanted." My eyes filled with tears. I blinked them away.

"I know, I know. I'm sorry. I'm glad I did though, because it showed me how important a real man is to you, and so I decided I can be that for you, and then we can be together forever. I can't imagine sharing you with someone like Pierce all my life. I covered my mouth from the shock of knowing what you needed and how I had to step up to my role for you."

"Honey, we'll always be together. We can get married. We can be two girls enjoying life. Pierce means nothing to me. He's just a fantasy, except in the flesh. You need to try him, and you'll see for yourself. I don't love Pierce. I just love how he makes me feel. The ultimate sex toy. A woman's impeccable male counterpart. A god for women. Try it."

"See? Ultimate, impeccable, a god—words that say nothing can compare. What femboy evolved into a girl could compete with that?"

I whined. "You can! I love you. Okay. I promise no more Pierce ever again. I can live without him. I can't live without you. Now, will you be my girlfriend?"

Riley's voice went panicky high. "No. Never. I'll be your boyfriend, though. And you'll love it." Riley looked at his hand and bent wrist he was using to emphasize his words, then made a fist and banged the table. He made his voice deep. "I'll be your man."

I reached across the table and grasped his hand, his pink fake fingernails still on. "Okay, honey. Whatever you like. As long as you're happy. I love you so much."

11

I managed to get Riley to leave the fake painted nails on by telling him they'd have to soak for a long time in acetone to melt them off. They'd wreck his nails if he tried to yank them off. I told him I wanted to go the art museum and not hang around waiting for his nails to soak all day.

Riley did his best to keep them hidden in his pockets as we made our way around the museum. He held his arm out for me to hold as we walked, just like a man and a woman would. He held doors for me and opened my car door.

He walked tall in his man boots and jeans and used a slightly deeper, more masculine voice when he talked. I was still slightly taller than him in my five-inch wedge heels. He said that was okay, though, because it was worth it to have me looking so good next to him in my heels. I was his arm candy.

When the day had ended, we decided to chill at our local hangout and see how the others had done so far.

"Avery! Look at you, girl!" Alex said from her seat at the table near the fireplace.

"Hey, Alex. Jamie!" I shouted as I came over to her. She now fully looked the part of a sissy bimbo slut. "You look fabulous, Jamie. Going man-hunting tonight?"

For sure. Being this way makes me crazy horny. I love it. Not sure I'd dress this way all the time, but after being all girl yesterday and being somewhat conservative about it, I thought I had to try this. Sit with us. Tell us what's been up. Riley, you look even less fem than I ever saw you before. Are you feeling sick?"

"No. I'm not sick! I'm a guy. Not a femboy. Not a girl. I'm a guy."

"If you say so." Jamie laughed a bimbo laugh. She turned to me. "Now you, Avery, look fabulous. You're such a natural. I love your wedge heels, denim skirt, and sheer suntan stockings. So fetching and such a pretty and casual day look."

"Thank you, Jamie. It feels natural to be like this now. I'm never going back. This is me. I just wish Riley would be the girl she is. You should have seen her last night. You can't tell, but her hair was styled and highlighted, and she looked fabulous."

Riley took a deep breath and looked away, unconsciously fixing his man bun, his long, painted nails glinting.

Jamie took Riley's hand and held it to get his attention. "Riley, what's wrong? Look at those pretty nails. Why are you fighting this, girl?"

Riley shook Jamie's hand away and put his hands under the table. "Don't call me girl. I'm a man. It's who I am. I just need to find some time to get rid of these darn nails."

I shook my head. "It's my fault, Jamie. I let Riley watch while I was pierced by Pierce last night. A real man. A hunk. Now Riley thinks she needs to be a man for me. It's all my fault. I'm an idiot."

Jamie looked back and forth at us. Riley was sheepish, and I felt sad. "Bummer. You know, Riley, you can't be who you aren't. It doesn't mean you can't be two girls in love. So what if Avery had a good lay last night? Maybe you should get one too, and it'll fix what's ailing you, once you have a real man demonstrate what an alluring woman you are."

Riley rolled his eyes and looked away; he crossed his legs and bounced a foot, and his fingers played with his stud earring. "I don't need a real man. I love Avery, and that's all I want. I want to be everything for her. That's all."

Jamie shook her blonde bimbo head. "No one can be everything to someone. That's unrealistic. Maybe you should try to be the girl you are and let a real man teach you how good it feels to have their passion for you deposited into you like Avery had. It'll make you feel whole and complete as a woman, knowing your allure to them, feeling their passion released deep inside you."

Riley's face turned red. "I don't want to talk about this anymore. Let's move on. Avery, honey, please tell Jamie to stop making me angry."

"Yes, dear. Jamie, please stop bothering Riley. Let's talk about something manly so she can feel masculine."

Jamie nodded and slapped her stockinged leg. "Good idea. So Riley, what teams do think will make it to the finals this year?" She bounced one of her legs over the other.

"I don't follow sports."

"Oh. Okay. Then what's your favorite vehicle? I love jeeps and can't wait to ride with the sides off and dressed like a bimbo. Girls look so hot in jeeps, don't you think?" She sipped her Cosmo and waited for Riley.

Riley sipped his beer and shrugged. "Hmm. Vehicles. I don't know. Anything that gets me from A to B is good. Something quiet and cute and not too big and noisy. You know. Maybe something like those little cars that look like sneakers. They're cute."

Jamie nodded. "Cute vehicles. Nice. That sounds very manly, Riley."

Riley rolled her eyes and slid her long-nailed hands up and down her jeans. "I can be very manly, Jamie. Tell her, Avery. Tell her how manly I can be. Help me here."

"Uh, yes. Of course, precious. Um, Avery made really good bacon the other day, and she cooks really well. She could be a chef."

"Stop calling me she, honey. Okay?"

"Right. He cooks well. A male chef. Oh, and he's really good at doing yard work. He loves planting flowers, and when I get the mower running for him, he always takes his girl shoes off and puts on his boy sneakers and mows the grass. A true gentleman."

Riley smiled. "Yeah. Yardwork. I love planting flowers and wearing my flower-planting gloves when I do."

"Flower-planting gloves?" Jamie asked.

"I wear pink rubber gloves when I plant to keep my nails clean. I love how tight they are and how long they make my hands look."

"I see. Pretty gloves. You use pretty gloves for other things too?"

"Well, when I rake or mow the grass or anything that might get me dirty or cause blisters, I do. I have an assortment of nice snug gloves in different colors to match my mood."

"That's good. Girls should take care of their hands. Don't want any calluses when they take care of their men's needs."

"I'm not a girl, and the only person I take care of is Avery. She's my girlfriend." Riley smiled at me and took my hand in hers. "I love Avery."

Jamie finished her Cosmo and stood in her stripper shoes. She slung on her cross-body purse and adjusted it between her breasts. "Well, girls. Don't know about you two, but I'm on a mission to find a real man tonight. Oh wait. We have one here. Riley." She squatted next to Riley and put her long-nailed hand on his head. "Hey, big boy, think you could show this girl a good time?" She ran her hand on his crotch. "Mama needs an injection, big boy. I can't feel it in your pink panties, though. Is it there?"

"Stop it, Jamie. You're not very stimulating, and they're not pink, they're pistachio with pink polka dots. I'm buying tighty-whities tomorrow. Avery, make him stop." Riley moved Jamie's hand off his crotch and crossed his legs, bouncing a foot. He tented his hands on a knee.

Jamie laughed and stood. "See you girls later!" She clattered away in her heels.

There we sat. Riley and Alex and me. Alex looked exceptionally nice as a girl too. I was sure Riley wanted it. The way he sat and the way he took Alex in, wishing to be like her. He wanted to be the girl again. This was stupid.

Riley looked at me. He could never be the real-man type of animalistic, divine deliverance he knew as Pierce. He knew it. Jamie knew it. Alex and I looked at Riley with pity in our eyes.

I slid my hand on Riley's leg. "You okay, honey? Jamie's gone now, and there's no one to taunt you."

"I know. Jamie's right, though. You're right. I'm masquerading this way, and I look at you two and know it even more. I want to be like the two of you. I'm a girl, not a guy. How can I be so stupid?"

Alex and I immediately burst into little whoops and claps. "Yea, Riley!" I kissed his cheek. "Let's blow this joint and get you dolled up. I want to change too, and then we can go to dinner and celebrate. I'll buy tonight. You bought last night. It's your turn to be pampered."

Riley leaned in and gave me a peck on the lips. Sheepishly she said, "Thank you." She looked at Alex, then whispered in my ear, "Sure, princess. Why not?"

I turned to Alex. "Alex, would you like to join us?" Alex was sipping her gin and tonic, looking prim and proper in her 1960s-style, baby blue swing dress—though much shorter than in the '60s, with pink flowers and revealing a lot of cleavage. Her hair was in a '60s curled bob. Her eyes lit up. "I'd love to. I was wondering what to do this evening."

"Delightful. I'll make reservations." I took my phone out while Alex and Riley chatted animatedly. "Done. We can pick you up, or you can meet us at our place and we can go together, or you can meet us there."

"Let's meet at your place. Can I come now? I walked here and was planning on doing some drinking tonight, so I don't want to drive anywhere."

Riley smiled and stood and held Alex's seat for her to stand. Alex stood, and Riley put her wrap on her and handed her her purse. "Ready, pretty lady?"

12

We went back home, I fixed Alex a drink, and Riley and I quickly did our makeup for an evening look, changed into a couple of beaded, V-neck-top minidresses with full, crinoline skirts in a baby blue—a shade that made my eyes pop—and a pistachio green for Riley that went stunningly well with her reddish highlighted hair.

Sheer suntan gartered stockings were held up with garter belts, again, baby blue for me and pistachio green for Riley. We both wore new strappy silver stilettos with fetishy high heels that made us walk in mincing steps. We had purses that matched our dresses and coordinated bows in our hair.

I felt like a princess as I put on my jewelry next to Riley, and we sprayed perfume all under and over us. We held hands, our purses slung on our shoulders as we did a final inspection before the full-length mirror. I took in Riley's beauty and couldn't help throbbing in my silky baby blue panties. "You're so sexy, honey. I love you." I gave her a peck on the lips.

She looked me up and down. "As are you. You're such a perfect lady. I love seeing you beam like that when you're in your true self." She pecked me and tugged my hand. "Let's go. Alex is waiting for us."

We stepped out in a clatter to the great room where Alex was perusing our array of pictures of the two of us. She turned as we entered and covered her mouth with her hand in its sheer glove. "Oh my, you two look stunning. What a gorgeous couple you make! I feel so underdressed."

Riley stepped over to her and fixed a stray lock of hair. "Nonsense. You're the perfect lady, Alex." She kissed her cheek. "Ready?"

We exited the house together, and Riley opened the car's back door for Alex to get in, then joined me up front. She crossed her legs and began mindlessly caressing her leg as she turned in her seat to be able to see Alex. "So Alex, tell us how it's been going evolving into the woman you've become?"

"It's been wonderful. I used to dress from time to time in private, but never to the degree of detail as now. It's like Jamie said, it's so liberating. It feels so natural and sensual and femininely proper. Are you two okay now? I mean, I heard the problems you were having, Riley. With Avery's interlude."

Riley nodded. "I'm fine now. I think." Riley turned to me. "Where are we going, honey?"

"The same place we were last night."

"What!?"

"Don't worry, honey. I'm not going to use Pierce. That's your role tonight. You can be the womanly one and provide a place for him to deposit his passion."

"Honey, no. I don't want to."

Alex leaned forward and stroked her hair. "Riley, you must. It's the proper thing for you to do to fully immerse yourself in being a woman. You simply must. It's heavenly. You two must have had that kind of sex before with each other, but with a real manly man, it's very special."

I nodded. "Yes, dear, you must. See? Alex agrees."

Riley shook her hair and fluffed it, resetting the bow while she composed her response. She took my hand off the console and squeezed it. "Honey, when was the last time you topped me?"

I thought about it, trying to remember. It was always Riley who topped me, mostly with a strap-on. "Umm, there must have been a time..."

Riley glanced at me. "Nope, I'm never going to be a bottom. Never. Don't want to. Don't need to. It's not my thing and it's still not my thing."

Alex gasped. "Oh Riley. That's so sad."

Riley turned to face her again. "It's not. Lots of people never do that. Men and women. I'm one of them. Just because I was a femboy doesn't mean I want to be penetrated like that. Is that bad? Does that make me a freak or something?"

Alex and I both shook our heads. I slid my hand on Riley's silky leg. "No honey. You aren't a freak. You're you. I'm so sorry I just never gave it a thought."

Alex leaned forward and stroked Riley's hair. "It's okay, honey. You aren't a freak. You're a beautiful woman."

I pulled up to the valet. We all got our things together as the valet opened Alex's door and helped her out. Riley and I exited and joined arms, and Alex followed us in.

We were seated by the fireplace. Pierce delivered glasses of water, a big grin on his face. I couldn't help but blush when I saw him. He knew how much I had enjoyed the other night.

"Ladies! So good to have you back. Avery, Riley, I see you have a new friend in your midst. A most beautiful friend, at that." He held his hand out to Alex. She placed hers in his, and he kissed the back of it. "I'm Pierce, and I'm here to give you a wonderful experience."

"Hello, Pierce. So nice to meet you."

Pierce's eyes took Alex in head to toe while he made sure to display the ripple of his pants to her beneath his towel. He caught her looking at it with her eyes wide.

Pierce smiled at her and said, "So Alex, I take it you know these girls very well. Are you a girl as special as they are?"

Riley nodded. "Yes, Pierce. She's just like us if you must know. She's very special. I think, though, that you should behave yourself and not ask such private questions like that."

Pierce stood at attention as if reprimanded. "My apologies. It's just so exciting to me to be honored to serve you all. Please. The first round is on me. I ask your forgiveness."

I smiled up at Pierce. "Oh, Pierce! You're forgiven. I understand your interests. You can't change a person's preferences. We're honored you're partial to us. Thank you for the drink. I think we'll all have the lady's passion."

He looked around the table, and Riley nodded. Alex looked up from the drink menu. "Please. That will be very fitting." She looked toward his crotch, but it was hidden by the towel on his arm. He nodded and left.

Alex leaned into us. "Oh... my... god... he's packing big time. What a catch. And he said he likes us? You must have been in heaven, Avery. He put that monster inside you?"

I leaned into Alex. "Deep, very, very, deep. It pierced my soul. It almost came out my throat! It was fantastic." I glanced at Riley, who was now looking sad. I took her hand and squeezed it. "But I'm all done with him. It's Riley I'm with forever." I kissed her lips lightly and tried to get her to smile.

She did and relaxed. "Alex, I'm sure you can have Pierce later if you want. So let's relax and enjoy a good meal."

Pierce brought the drinks and placed them in front of us. He angled his presentation to Alex, and I'm sure she got to see him hard in his pants because her eyes lit up, and she didn't take them off it until he left with a grin on his face.

I toasted. "To being the women we were always meant to be." We all clinked and sipped daintily. Alex sipped again and then again. Half her drink was gone.

We all chatted, had oysters, and Alex had three more lady's passions to our one more before we ordered dinner.

Pierce must have done his flashing trick because Alex's hand went over her mouth when he did, and he turned and fled quickly, the towel covering it as he disappeared.

Alex uncovered her mouth. She took Riley's hand. "Oh, honey. You have to have him. Even if you've never had one, it would be a shame to pass up such a god."

Riley laughed. "No thanks, Alex. He's all yours. Unless, of course, Avery wants some. He can finish more than once." Riley turned to me and shrugged. "I can bear it now, I guess. If you want it."

"You'll just be mad at me and try to be a man again, and I already had that fantasy fulfilled anyway. The only person I want to feel in me is you... or, uh..." She covered her mouth, her eyes wide, "You wearing my intimate friend, Bruno the Impaler."

She kissed my lips and laughed. "No problem. I like wearing Bruno."

Riley ran her hand over my silky stockinged leg and looked around. She slid her hand up under the fluffy crinoline and searched to find me hard and set free of my panties in the fluff of the crinoline. "You naughty girl, Avery. You're hard in your nest."

"I sure am. Just enjoying being with you and now, thinking about Bruno... mmm." Riley kissed my lips and caressed my leg with her long-nailed hand.

Alex, half toasted but still looking the proper 1960s wife watched us, smiling. She was just a little toasty with high pink cheeks and bright eyes, legs crossed and high heel bouncing, with her hand in her lap moving almost imperceptibly but steadily as she increased her anticipation. She glanced around looking for Pierce to reappear with dessert. "So, how does this work? Do I go out back or to a car?"

I shook my head. "No. The storage room. It has a table. You won't need the table, though. You'll be like a blow-up doll to him. He can carry you around and do it to you."

Alex's hand moved more under the table, her dress making swishing sounds with each stroke. "Oh my." She took a deep breath.

I leaned into Riley. "Isn't this exciting? I feel bad for you that I can't give that to you." I slid my hand under her dress and wrapped her hardness, now free of her panties, in the soft crinoline. "Mmm, I guess it is exciting, huh, baby? You're hard and free in the nest too." I stroked her.

She nodded, looking around. "Don't worry. Pierce is the only one who might see us. No one else is around."

I stroked her faster and kissed her lips. I whispered to her, "Want to watch Alex?"

I watched you last time, but it didn't do anything for me. It made me afraid. But this time, I think it would be fun seeing that it's Alex and not you."

"Really? I thought you came watching me."

She shook her head, almost embarrassed, and I could feel her begin to soften in my hand. "I'm so sorry, sweetie. Forget that. Think of Alex instead and the gift we're giving her tonight. Look how excited she is." Alex was obviously fully aroused and practically glowing in anticipation. "Look how pretty Alex is and how much she wants it." Riley became firm in my hand again. "We can both watch and enjoy her, okay?"

Riley began stroking me again through my nest. "Thatta girl. Make me feel nice too." I looked around, and the coast was still clear. All three of us were feeling nice and being caressed. I took my hand away and moved Riley's to herself. "It'll be less obvious if we do ourselves. Make yourself feel nice, honey." She began to stroke herself, and her mouth cracked open, her breaths coming swifter. "That's it, feel how pretty you are," I murmured to her.

I leaned back, and we all looked at each other as our hands worked ourselves and our arousal built and we waited. Our eyes drifted from one to the other, enjoying our mutual pleasure and sharing it with each other. We got lost in looking longingly at each other's made-up, sexy eyes, revealing the mutual, sensual, feminine pleasure we were feeling.

Plates hit the table. "What a lovely group of ladies waiting patiently and building up an appetite for the final course." We all stopped abruptly. "No, no, please, ladies. The place is empty. Keep your engines running while you enjoy dessert. It's a pleasure for me to see you all in such a pleasant state." Pierce smiled at each of us in turn. "Lovely. Beautiful. Riley, please, start again."

I did as I gazed lovingly into his eyes.

He smiled and nodded to the others to do the same. They started again fervently. "Thank you, ladies. I'm honored. Please keep going." He looked at each of us in turn and nodded approval as we all continued and he watched for a few moments. He left and we stared at the magnificently presented bananas.

We switched hands and continued to caress ourselves while we ate quietly, all of us in some sort of out-of-body experience. We ate about half before we stopped and just sat there, caressing ourselves and enjoying each other's pleasure.

Pierce came out again. This time though, we saw him coming and we didn't stop. He knelt next to Alex on one knee. "Lovely lady, if you desire, I would love the honor of making love to you. If you approve of me, I'd like to offer you my hand in marriage, and when and if you approve, I can make you my bride."

Alex's left hand covered her mouth daintily. "Oh my, I don't know what to say."

"No hurry. Now the checks have been taken care of. If you'd like to join me for a moment before you leave, I can lead the way." He turned to Riley and me, "And of course, you ladies are welcome to join us as well."

Alex stared at us, her painted eyes wide open, her hand over her mouth. I grasped her free hand on the table while she continued stroking herself mindlessly. "Let's go. It's time. Think about marriage later. Be his temporary bride for now."

She stood and Pierce took her arm and led her to the storeroom. We followed them.

Pierce unveiled his manliness and leaned back against the table while he stroked it. "Who will have the appetizer so I can be my best for my bride?"

Riley and I looked at each other. Riley ran his hand over my hair. "Go, honey. Do it for me. Have him inside you again. I'll be okay. Really. Do it."

I looked at Riley, confused, and shook my head. She grabbed my hand and wrapped it around her hard shaft and made me stroke it. "See? I'm really hard at the thought now. I want you to have it for me. I want to see you in heaven again. I can give you this gift without me feeling bad like before. I've evolved and I love you and I want to see you satisfied. I know now it's my gift to both of us, and I want to see it so badly."

Riley led me to the table and boosted me onto it. She spread my legs and lifted my dress, then pulled my panties aside and motioned Pierce to me. She handed a condom from her purse to

Pierce, and he slid it over his glorious pole. I kissed her cheek and held her close to me. "Stroke yourself for me, Riley. Show me how good this is for you."

Riley lifted the hem of her dress and wrapped a single layer of crinoline around her shaft and stroked it with a thumb and forefinger with her pinky out. "Good girl—now you can guide Pierce into me and then begin that again."

She guided Pierce into me, and he went into full gear. He lifted me up, and I held fast to Riley, my head on her shoulder, sniffing the perfume on her neck while I whimpered. Pierce impaled me over and over. I dropped my hand to my side and fished for Riley's shaft and found it.

It was rock-hard, and I wrapped the crinoline and my fingers around it gently so she could slide in the smooth fabric. Riley thrusted into my hand while Pierce thrusted into me. I whispered to Riley in between Pierce's voice-stopping thrusts, "That's my good girl... huh, slide that in my hand while Pierce shoves his into me... uh, my god yes... huh. Do what he does to me, but to my hand and your pretty crinoline wrapping."

Riley whimpered as she thrusted in little jerks; I could feel her excitement in my palm. She felt so cute. "My god, Avery... you're so hot. This feels so right. I love you this way."

"I love you... uh, huh... I love you, Riley." I kissed her head and turned to Pierce. "Pierce, now. Put your seed in me and make Riley and me end this before we both pass out."

I felt Pierce swell inside me. "That's it, Pierce. I feel you pulsing inside me now." I spurted all over my dress while Riley shook and clung tight to me as she thrusted like an adolescent on a pillow, whimpering and shaking. Wetness filled her crinoline and my hand, making me feel such love for and from her. It felt even better than Pierce did.

We both slumped when we were done, and Pierce retracted his thunderbolt. We moved aside and off the table onto our wobbly heels, helping each other to stand, and Alex hurriedly climbed onto the table while Pierce replaced the condom.

Alex was ready, her dress lifted, her 1960s girdle holding up her stockings, her tiny hairless shaft bobbing on its own in the air before her. Her face showed her thrill as she watched Pierce approach. She greedily grabbed his shaft and tugged him to her. She forced herself onto him with a gasp, a grimace, and a grunt. "Yes! God, yes! Breed your bride!" she said into his face. "Do it with passion. Show me you're worthy to be my husband."

Riley and I stood and watched as Pierce made his most concerted effort so far. Alex was tossed to and fro like a blow-up doll, her high heels flailed with each thrust, her head snapped back and forth, and her eyes rolled in her head. The whimpers and squeaks of a little lady issued from her glossy red lips while she bit her pink tongue, and her eyes rolled in her head like a broken doll.

I glanced at Riley, who had her phone out and was videoing the show while she rubbed the front of her dress with her hand. I knelt down and turned her to the side so I could glance at them from the corner of my eyes while I lifted her dress and took her into my mouth, soon bringing her once again to her full hardness. Pierce was lasting and probably could last forever if poor little Alex could take it.

I feared Alex might fall apart like a toy doll with all the action Pierce was providing her. He wrapped an arm around her, and her legs wrapped and locked around his waist. His other hand cradled her head, and he looked into her eyes, grunting with each thrust, his face contorted as if in rage.

Alex whimpered and squeaked. After some time—much longer that I'd thought she would endure—Alex begged, "Oh god! Yes, Pierce. Please fill me with your seed before I die. Please do it now. Use me up and give it all to me."

He stuffed her several more times, then shoved it deep and held it there, releasing his energy into her. He peppered her neck with kisses as her legs flailed behind him in spasms of her uncontrollable release.

Riley gripped my head tight and deposited a few small shots into my mouth as she shuddered on her high heels. I held her from falling while I swallowed. I stood and kissed her, giving her back her own fluids. She swallowed them down and kissed me deeply. She dropped to her knees and took me into her mouth, and I released into her face instantly. She helped me to stand. We rearranged ourselves and looked to Alex.

Alex stood next to Pierce, smiling broadly and proudly; she nestled against him, and his arm wrapped around her. I said, "So, you two. Are you a couple now?"

Pierce looked down at Alex and rubbed her back. "Only if the lady deems me worthy. I don't want to pressure her, but she's the type of evolved woman I've been looking for all my life. A very special, very evolved woman. Like you two, but—please don't take offense—more my style. What do you say, Alex?"

"Uh, gosh… This is too fast. I know I've..." she motioned to us, "we've all evolved so much recently. I just want to take the time to feel it all out a little. Is that okay, Pierce? Honey?"

Pierce laughed, nodded, and gave her a bear hug, lifting her up off the floor. "Absolutely, my lady." He put her down and looked at us. "And you two are welcome in my restaurant anytime, and your meals and drinks will always be free. It's my gift to you both for bringing Alex into my life, whether we marry or not. However, I will be hers and hers alone. I will not share myself should she commit to me. Sorry if that disappoints either of you."

We all looked at each other, and Riley and I ran to Alex and Pierce to have a group hug. Riley stepped back and grabbed Pierce's hand. "Thank you, Pierce. Thank you for your role in helping us all evolve into the ladies we always were inside and for showing us our own truths. I think we'll all be friends for life. Even if my wife can't have you anymore. Right, Avery?"

"Wife? Oh yes, Riley. I'd love nothing more than to have you as my wife and girlfriend for life—and be friends with these two. I'm so happy you've evolved with me to become who we are and share it for life. I'll miss Pierce, but I'll be just fine with good old Bruno too."

Riley looked into my eyes lovingly and ran her long-nailed fingers through my hair. She kissed the nape of my neck. She wrapped my hand around her crinoline-covered now descending shaft. Looking deeply and longingly into my eyes, she said quietly, "What we did with Pierce was so nice for both of us. Why just use Bruno? Maybe Pierce has a brother, honey? If not, two pretty girls like us could surely find a replacement for Pierce."

"Oh Riley, my love. I don't need any more than you. I did love your involvement and how much you enjoyed it. Having you making love to my grip made me feel so loved and thrilled to have you as your passion mounted and you showed me how good it was for you."

"I truly did love it, Avery. You were so hot, sexy, and powerful, the way you made Pierce give it all to you. I couldn't help but be a part of it while he drove you to heaven and you held me close to you. I could feel your joy, and it gave me passion. It made me feel proud to be able to be there with you. It was overwhelmingly exciting and gratifying to be a part of."

"That is so sweet. You're such a cute girlfriend and soon-to-be wife, but good old Bruno will do from now on."

"Oh...okay, honey," Riley said, but she actually looked a little disappointed. Her head drooped.

"Are you okay, sweetie?"

"Yes, honey. Uh... but... I, uh..." She looked up wide eyed. "...I'd love to find you another... if you'd allow me to of course."

"Oh sweetie. Don't worry your pretty head about it." I patted her head.

Her eyes looked like they were ready to tear up. She blinked quickly and took a deep breath. She grabbed both of my hands and looked into my eyes. "But Avery...I guess...I guess it's like me massaging your legs, which you like so much and thank me for, but I enjoy incredibly. I mean...being there with you while you let me make love to your hand like that while he makes love to you, with us both finishing like that together. I mean. I felt so loved and connected to you and your pleasure...and I loved being with you, admiring the powerful woman you are while you reap your reward from a real manly man. It's *very* exciting for me. I guess... I'm being selfish again honey. For me, it's better than massaging your legs even. Have I evolved maybe?"

"Hmm...Yes, you have. In your special way. You're the perfect spouse. Let's just enjoy ourselves for a while, and maybe if you're a good girl and things come our way someday, we can do something like that again.

"Oh god! Thank you soo much!" She jumped up and down in her heels and clapped her hands like a little girl."

I laughed. "Okay honey let's go home and you can do that in my hand again and I'll narrate for you and tell you how good it will be for me with my next manly man. Okay, princess?" I kissed her forehead and patted her head.

Riley grinned ear to ear and rolled her eyes. "Thanks, sweetie. Let's go do that and get to sleep! Tomorrow we have to see how the other girls did, and then after a quick dinner, I want to take you clubbing and show off my trophy wife. Maybe we should dress like bimbos! For sure you should at least. We need to get you out there for others to see and enjoy. I can't wait to be there with you and a guy like that again." She giggled and covered her mouth.

"Okay, dear." I patted her head, kissed her forehead, and took her by the hand. Oh well. Be careful what you fantasize about. All things evolve.

53

If you enjoyed this book, it would be great if you could leave a review and tell a friend about it, or blog it out. Thanks!
Barb and Thom
For more of books, both fiction and non-fiction, go to:
Amazon:
http://www.amazon.com/Barbara-Deloto/e/B00J21HWA4/